For Martin,
Lil, Mimi, and
Debbie Pope

ALADDIN PAPERBACKS

Kitten for
a Day

by Ezra Jack Keats

Are you a kitten?

Uh huh--I think so.

O.K. Follow us!

Lap,lap,lap

Splash!

Lick,lick,lick

Slurp!

Meeeeoooow!

Meee...rrruff!

Ooops!

Eeeeek!

Thump!

Sorry!

Puppy,
come home
right now!

Next time,
let's all
be puppies!

First Aladdin Paperbacks edition 1993

Aladdin Paperbacks
An imprint of Simon & Schuster Children's Publishing Division
1230 Avenue of the Americas
New York, NY 10020

Printed in Hong Kong
10 9 8 7 6 5 4 3 2

Library of Congress Cataloging-in-Publication Data
Keats, Ezra Jack.
    Kitten for a day / by Ezra Jack Keats.
        p.   cm.
    Summary: A puppy joins a litter of kittens in their fun and games for one day.
    ISBN 0-689-71737-7
    [1. Dogs—Fiction.   2. Cats—Fiction.]   I. Title.
    [PZ7.K2253Ki   1993]
    [E]—dc20   92-40563